AMERICAN HOLIDAYS

★ ★

Columbus Day

Rennay Craats

Weigl Publishers Inc.

Published by Weigl Publishers Inc.
350 5th Avenue, Suite 3304
New York, NY USA 10118-0069
Web site: www.weigl.com

Library of Congress Cataloging-in-Publication Data

Craats, Rennay.
  Columbus Day / Rennay Craats.
      p. cm. -- (American holidays)
Summary: Examines the history Columbus Day and describes some of the
ways that this holiday is celebrated.
Includes bibliographical references and index.
  ISBN 1-59036-106-7 (lib. bdg. : alk. paper) — ISBN 1-59036-164-4 (pbk.)
 1. Columbus Day--Juvenile literature. 2. Columbus,
Christopher--Juvenile literature. 3. America--Discovery and
exploration--Spanish--Juvenile literature. [1. Columbus Day. 2.
Columbus, Christopher. 3. America--Discovery and exploration--Spanish.
4. Holidays.] I. Title. II. American holidays (Mankato, Minn.)
  E120.C88 2004
  394.264--dc21
                                    2003003953

Printed in the United States of America
1 2 3 4 5 6 7 8 9 0 07 06 05 04 03

Project Coordinator Tina Schwartzenberger **Substantive Editor** Heather C. Hudak
Design Terry Paulhus **Layout** Susan Kenyon **Photo Researcher** Barbara Hoffman

Contents

Introduction

★ ★

Christopher Columbus believed Earth was round.

On the second Monday of October, American families celebrate Columbus Day. This holiday celebrates the day that Christopher Columbus discovered the Americas. Columbus and his crew landed on San Salvador, Central America, on October 12, 1492. Columbus was the first European to reach the Americas.

Christopher Columbus was courageous. While most people believed Earth was flat, Columbus believed Earth was round. It was thought that ships would fall off the "edge of the world." Columbus disagreed, and sailed west in search of Asia. Instead, he found the Americas. Columbus became wealthy and famous. He believed he had discovered a new route to Asia. When he died in 1506, he did not know that he had discovered the Americas.

DID YOU KNOW?

Christopher Columbus never explored the land that became the United States of America. He landed on the island of Puerto Rico.

s a young adult, Christopher Columbus worked as a messenger and a sailor on
ifferent ships.

Dreams of the Sea

★ ★

Columbus promised to find a faster route to Asia.

DID YOU KNOW?

Christopher Columbus studied for many hours to become a captain. To learn all he could about the world, he studied *The Bible*, map making, geography, and the writings of other explorers.

Christopher Columbus was born in Genoa, Italy, in 1451. As a child, he worked with his mother and father as a wool weaver. At age 14, he began a seafaring career. At the time, Europeans sailed around Africa to reach Asia. Columbus believed that a faster route to Asia could be found by sailing west.

For years, Columbus asked the leaders of many European countries to pay for his trip. In return, he promised to find a faster route to Asia. No one was willing to pay for his trip. In 1492, Columbus talked to King Ferdinand V and Queen Isabella I of Spain. They gave him money for his voyage. On August 3, 1492, three ships—*The Nina*, *The Pinta*, and *The Santa Maria*—and ninety sailors set sail from Spain.

Christopher Columbus promised to bring King Ferdinand V and Queen Isabella I of Spain gold, spices, and silk from Asia.

New World

★ ★

Columbus claimed San Salvador for Spain.

DID YOU KNOW?

Christopher Columbus formed a **colony** near Cape Isabella, Dominican Republic. This was the first European settlement in the New World.

When Christopher Columbus and his crew finally reached land, they believed they were in Asia. They dressed in their best clothes to meet the local leaders. The people they met were not Asian. They were the **indigenous peoples** of South America. The sailors had landed in the Bahamas, on an island named Guanahani. Columbus renamed the area San Salvador. He claimed it for Spain.

The crew continued to sail around the land they thought was Asia. They landed on the island of Cuba. Columbus thought they had reached Japan. They sailed further to the islands of Española, which are now the Dominican Republic and Haiti. After losing one of his ships, the remaining two ships sailed back to Spain in 1493.

On his first voyage, Christopher Columbus visited the islands of the Bahamas, Cuba, and Española.

On November 3, 1493, Christopher Columbus discovered the island of Guadeloupe.

Words of Wisdom

★ ★

Sea captains such as Christopher Columbus wrote in journals every day.

In the 1400s and 1500s, many sailors wrote about their voyages. Since so much of the sea and land had not been explored, it was important to keep a record of each trip. Sea captains such as Christopher Columbus wrote in journals every day. Columbus wrote about the direction his ships sailed, the winds and other weather conditions, what he saw, and what was happening aboard the ship. His journals provided the details of his discovery.

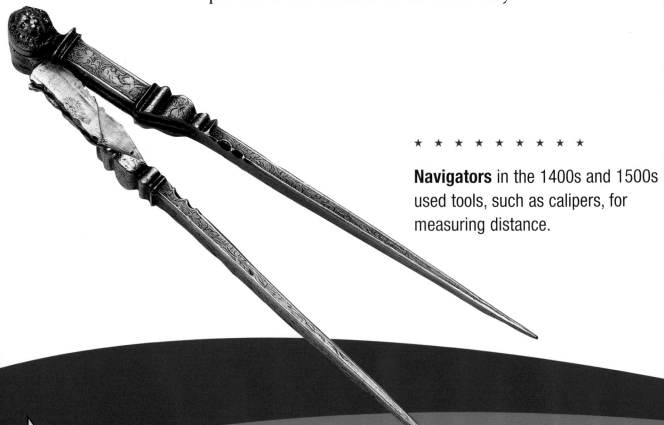

★ ★ ★ ★ ★ ★ ★ ★ ★

Navigators in the 1400s and 1500s used tools, such as calipers, for measuring distance.

Journal Entry

*The land was first seen by a sailor called Rodrigo de Triana, although the Admiral at ten o'clock that evening standing on the quarter-deck saw a light, but so small a body that he could not affirm it to be land. At two o'clock in the morning the land was discovered, at two **leagues'** distance. They took in sail and remained under the square-sail lying to till day, which was Friday, when they found themselves near a small island, one of the Lucayos, called, in the Indian language, Guanahani.*

—Christopher Columbus

Columbus and his crew set foot on land on October 12, 1492, after thirty-six days of sailing.

Creating the Holiday

★ ★

In 1792, New York held a ceremony to honor Columbus.

DID YOU KNOW?

The Pledge of Allegiance to the American flag was first said in public schools during a Columbus Day celebration in 1892.

Christopher Columbus's discovery was not celebrated in the United States for 300 years. In 1792, New York held a ceremony to honor Columbus. Soon after, the city of Washington was named the District of Columbia in honor of Columbus's discovery. People of Italian heritage living in New York City wanted to officially honor Columbus. They were very proud of him. In 1866, they organized events to celebrate Columbus and his discovery of the Americas. The next year, more Italian organizations across the country held celebrations, too. People of Italian heritage in San Francisco were the first to name their celebration Columbus Day.

The first official Columbus Day celebrations took place 400 years after Columbus discovered the Americas. On October 12, 1892, President Benjamin Harrison asked all U.S. citizens to remember Columbus and his discovery. In 1934, President Franklin Roosevelt made October 12, Columbus Day, an official celebration. Since 1971, the national holiday has been celebrated on the second Monday in October. During this long weekend, families and friends across the U.S. gather to celebrate Columbus Day.

September 1934, President Franklin Roosevelt made an official announcement asking the United States to observe October 12, Columbus Day, as a national holiday.

Celebrating Today

★ ★

Many Columbus Day parades have an Italian theme.

DID YOU KNOW?

Some people do not think Columbus Day should be celebrated. They do not believe that Columbus was a hero since the discovery of the Americas led to the death of many Native Peoples.

Since Christopher Columbus was Italian, many Columbus Day celebrations involve people of Italian heritage. Many Columbus Day parades have an Italian theme. These celebrations often feature Italian-American celebrities and traditional dancing and music. Christopher Columbus, his culture, and traditions are honored. Today, many U.S. citizens celebrate the second Monday in October by enjoying the sights, sounds, and tastes of local Italian culture.

Some people celebrate Columbus Day at parades and festivals. Most major cities host parades or festivals during the holiday weekend. Some people have small neighborhood festivals and parades. Many spend the day relaxing with their friends and family.

Many Columbus Day celebrations feature traditional Italian foods, such as crusty bread, olive oil, and prosciutto—a salted ham.

Americans Celebrate

Columbus Day is celebrated across the United States. This map shows a few events that take place each year on the second Monday in October.

San Francisco, California

Every year, the biggest Columbus Day parade in the West takes place in San Francisco. The Italian Heritage Parade offers food, floats, and other activities such as car shows.

0   100   200   300 miles

About 100,000 people attend the Columbus Day Parade in Chicago. The floats, bands, and local and state celebrities form a parade that is more than 1 mile long.

New York City hosts the biggest Columbus Day celebration in the U.S. New York's large Italian-American community honors Christopher Columbus and the discovery of the Americas.

New York City, New York

Ocean County, New Jersey

Chicago, Illinois

Each year, Ocean County, New Jersey, hosts a Columbus Day Parade and Italian Festival. The celebration honors Columbus's discovery and Italian heritage in the United States. The parade is filled with clowns, floats, and bands.

In Miami, people celebrate Columbus Day on the water. The annual Columbus Day **Regatta** has drawn sailors since 1954. To honor Columbus, sailors compete in a race in Biscayne Bay.

Miami, Florida

Holiday Symbols

American citizens have honored Christopher Columbus in many ways. Several cities in such states as Georgia, Ohio, Nebraska, and Mississippi have been named after the sea captain. **Monuments** across the United States honor Christopher Columbus, his voyages, and his discovery of the Americas.

Walla Walla, Washington
A statue of Christopher Columbus has stood in Walla Walla, Washington, since 1911. It is one of the oldest statues made to honor the navigator on the West Coast. Italian immigrant farmers paid for this piece of art. The statue stands 7 feet tall on a 12-foot **pedestal**. A dedication to Columbus and his voyage to the Americas is written on the pedestal.

★ ★ ★ ★ ★ ★ ★ ★ ★

The Christopher Columbus statue in Walla Walla, Washington, was a gift to the city from the Italian community.

Phoenix, Arizona

Phoenix, Arizona, presented its citizens with a bronze statue of Christopher Columbus in 1992. The monument was built to honor Columbus. The public first saw the statue on the 500th anniversary of Columbus's first voyage to the New World. The statue stands 7 feet high and weighs 2,000 pounds. Some people have **protested** the statue. It has also been **vandalized.** Since 1992, the statue has been moved to five different locations.

Los Angeles, California

A statue in Los Angeles, California, celebrates Christopher Columbus's voyages. This statue shows the sea captain holding a map in one hand. Columbus is portrayed telling Spain's king and queen the plans for his voyage. The life-sized bronze statue was made in Italy.

Further Research

Many books and Web sites offer information about Christopher Columbus and Columbus Day. Here are a few resources to help you learn more.

Web Sites

Find out more about Christopher Columbus at:
www.sunniebunniezz.com/ holiday/columbus.htm

Learn about America before Columbus arrived at:
http://lcweb.loc.gov/exhibits/1492

Books

deRubertis, Barbara. *Columbus Day: Let's Meet Christopher Columbus.* New Jersey: Kane Press, 1996.

Fradin, Dennis Brindell. *Columbus Day.* New York: Enslow Publishers, Inc., 1990.

Crafts and Recipes

Juice Box Sailboat

There are many fun crafts you can create for Columbus Day. For example, using an empty juice box, you can make a small sailboat boat similar to *The Nina*, *The Pinta*, or *The Santa Maria*. Cut a rectangular sail from a plastic milk jug or pop bottle. Use stickers and markers to decorate the sail. You may also decorate the juice box if you wish. Make a small hole in the center of each end of the sail. Slide a drinking straw through the holes. Cut a small opening in the center of the juice box. Insert the straw and sail inside the opening. Your juice box sailboat is now finished. Try racing your boat in a large puddle.

Mapmaker

Unlike most sailors of his time, Columbus did not use navigational tools. Instead, he drew what he saw on his travels. Pretend that you are an explorer. Make a map of your home, classroom, local shopping mall, or playground. Draw pictures of the items in these places, such furniture. Have you placed each item in the right location?

Columbus Day Recipe

Make a Columbus Day Boat

Ingredients:

eighteen marshmallows

nine maraschino cherries

vanilla ice cream

butterscotch syrup

Equipment:

ice cream scoop	spoon	markers
twelve toothpicks	can opener	scissors
three plates	paper	tape

1. Place three scoops of ice cream on each plate. Spoon butterscotch syrup on top of each scoop.
2. Make nine sandwiches by placing a cherry between two marshmallows. Use a toothpick to hold your sandwich together.
3. Put one toothpick in each scoop of ice cream.
4. Cut a rectangular piece of paper and tape it onto another toothpick. This will be your boat's flag. Use markers to decorate the flag.
5. Place the toothpick flag on top of the middle marshmallow on each plate. You have made ice cream copies of *The Nina, The Pinta*, and *The Santa Maria*.

HUNTINGTON CITY-TOWNSHIP
PUBLIC LIBRARY
200 W. Market Street
Huntington IN 46750

Holiday Quiz

What have you learned about Columbus Day? See if you can answer the following questions. Check your answers on the next page.

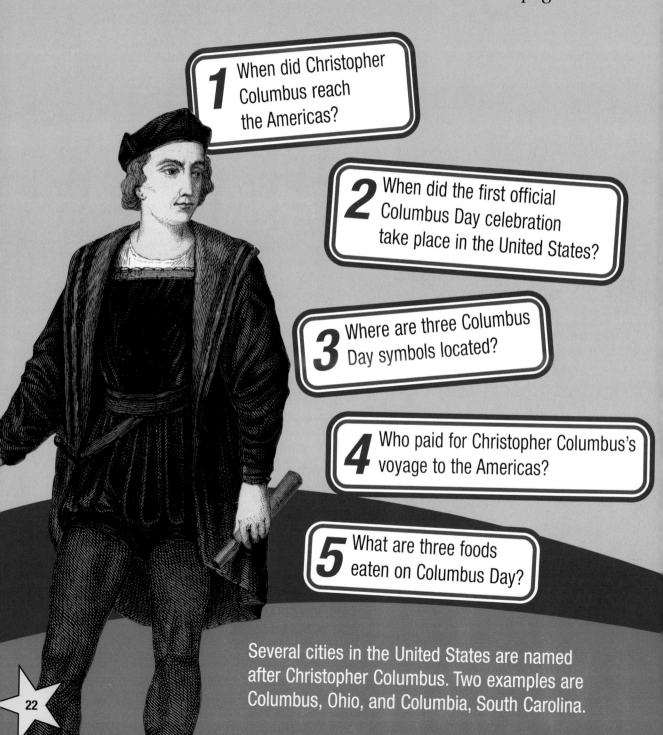

1 When did Christopher Columbus reach the Americas?

2 When did the first official Columbus Day celebration take place in the United States?

3 Where are three Columbus Day symbols located?

4 Who paid for Christopher Columbus's voyage to the Americas?

5 What are three foods eaten on Columbus Day?

Several cities in the United States are named after Christopher Columbus. Two examples are Columbus, Ohio, and Columbia, South Carolina.

Fascinating Facts

★ Christopher Columbus and his brother Bartholomew were governors of a colony that Christopher formed in Santa Domingo. In 1499, both men were arrested, **shackled**, and sent back to Spain. The king and queen **pardoned** the two men.

★ Columbus's second voyage had 17 ships and 1,500 men.

★ Although Christopher Columbus discovered the Americas, they were not named after him. They were named after an Italian explorer named Amerigo Vespucci.

★ Christopher Columbus wanted to reach Asia so he could become rich. Europeans wanted the many spices and valuable goods found in Asia.

Quiz Answers:
1. Christopher Columbus first reached the Americas on October 12, 1492.
2. The first official Columbus Day celebration took place on October 12, 1892.
3. Columbus Day symbols are located in Phoenix, Arizona, Los Angeles, California, and Walla Walla, Washington.
4. King Ferdinand V and Queen Isabella I paid for Columbus's voyage.
5. Italian foods, such as crusty bread, olive oil, and prosciutto are eaten on Columbus Day.

Glossary

colony: an area that is ruled by a more powerful country

indigenous peoples: first people to inhabit a place

leagues: an old measure of distance equal to about 3 miles

monuments: large objects made of stone and meant to honor someone or something

navigator: the person who directs a ship

pardoned: forgiven

pedestal: the long column on which a statue sits

protested: showing disapproval for something

regatta: organized boat or yacht races

shackled: being held prisoner with iron rings joined by a chain around the wrists and ankles

vandalized: purposely damaged or destroyed by human activity

Index